This book belongs to

_____

I celebrated World Book Day 20
with this brilliant gift from my local bookseller,
Hodder Children's Books and *Enid Blyton*.

Enid Blyton

THE FAMOUS FIVE

Good Old Timmy and Other Stories

Hodder
Children's
Books

HODDER CHILDREN'S BOOKS

Good Old Timmy first published in Great Britain in 1956
in *Enid Blyton's Magazine Annual Number 3*
A Lazy Afternoon first published in Great Britain in 1954
in *Enid Blyton's Magazine Annual Number 1*
When Timmy Chased the Cat first published in Great Britain in 1957
in *Enid Blyton's Magazine Annual Number 4*

This edition published 2017 by Hodder and Stoughton

1 3 5 7 9 10 8 6 4 2

Enid Blyton ® The Famous Five ®
Enid Blyton's signature is a Registered Trademark of Hodder and Stoughton Limited
Text copyright © Hodder and Stoughton Limited
Illustrations copyright © Hodder and Stoughton Limited
Illustrated by Laura Ellen Anderson

A CIP catalogue record for this book is available from the British Library.

ISBN 9781444937190
Export ISBN 9781444938227

Printed and bound in Great Britain by CPI Group (UK) Ltd, Croydon, CR0 4YY

The paper and board used in this book are made from wood from responsible sources.

The Hachette Children's Group would like to thank
Holmen Paper, Hallsta Mill, Sweden and Paper Management Services
for their contribution to the paper used for this World Book Day printing.

Hodder Children's Books
An imprint of
Hachette Children's Group
Part of Hodder and Stoughton
Carmelite House
50 Victoria Embankment
London EC4Y 0DZ

An Hachette UK Company
www.hachette.co.uk
www.hachettechildrens.co.uk

CONTENTS

GOOD OLD
TIMMY

Chapter 1

'Aren't you ready to come down to the beach and swim, Anne?' yelled George, standing at the bottom of the stairs. 'We're all waiting for you. HURRY UP!'

The study door flew open and Mr Kirrin, George's father, appeared.

'Georgina! Will you stop shouting all day long? How can I work? For pity's sake, clear out of the house.'

'We're just going, Dad – and we're taking a picnic lunch so we won't be disturbing you for some time. I know you're on a big job – it's bad luck it's holiday time and we're here!'

He grunted and disappeared into his study. George's mother appeared with two big bags of sandwiches.

'Oh dear – was that your father shouting again?' she said. 'Never mind! He doesn't mean to be bad-tempered – but he really is on a big job at the moment, and he's trying to get some figures for the scientist he's working with, a Professor Humes, who's staying in Kirrin – at the Rollins Hotel. Now – here are your sandwiches – and biscuits and apples – and you can take some bottles of ginger beer out of the larder.'

Just then Anne raced down the stairs, and the Five, all in their swimming things, went off to the beach to swim and laze and play games on the sands.

Only three people were there – two men and a lonely-looking boy. Julian found a shaded cave and put the food on a shelf of rock.

'What about a swim straight away?' he said. 'Look – Timmy's off to rub noses with that dog we saw yesterday – the big ugly one we didn't much like. He belongs to those two men. They're not much to look at either! I wouldn't like to meet them on a dark night!'

'Well, Timmy seems to like their dog all right,' said George, staring at the two dogs sniffing at one another, then tearing along the sands together, barking happily.

Chapter 2

'Look,' said Dick, 'there's that kid coming along the beach again. Shall we ask him to come swimming with us – he seems to be all on his own. Look out, kid – don't get knocked over by our dog!'

Timmy had come racing up joyfully, chasing the other dog, and the boy went sprawling as they galloped round him. Timmy turned in surprise and saw the boy rolling over and over on the sand. He gave an apologetic bark, and ran to the small boy, licking and sniffing at him.

The boy was terrified of Timmy. He began to scream in terror, and Julian ran to him.

'He's only making friends, he's only saying he's sorry he knocked you over, he won't hurt you! Come on, get up – we were just going to ask you to come and swim with us.'

'Oh,' said the boy, and stood up, shaking the sand off himself. He looked to be about nine or ten, and small for his age. 'Well – thanks. I'd like to swim with you. I'm Oliver Humes, and I'm staying at the Rollins Hotel.'

'Then your dad must be a friend of our uncle,' said Dick. 'He's called Kirrin – Quentin Kirrin – and he's a scientist. So is your dad, isn't he?'

'Yes. A very good one too,' said Oliver proudly. 'But he's worried this morning.'

'Why? What's up?' said George.

'Well – he's working on something important,' said Oliver, 'and this morning he had a horrible letter. It said that unless Dad agreed to give the writer information he wanted about what Dad was working on, he'd – he'd kidnap me!'

Chapter 3

'Oh rubbish!' said Julian. 'Don't you
worry about that! We'll tell our dog
Timmy to look after you. Just look at him
playing with that ugly great mongrel.
Timmy's a mongrel too – but we think
he's beautiful!'

'I think he's too big,' said Oliver, fearfully,
as Timmy came running up, panting.

The other dog went back to the two men,
who had just whistled for him.

'Come on – let's swim,' said Dick.

'I can't swim,' said Oliver. 'I wish you'd
teach me.'

'Right. We will when we've had our swim,'

said Anne. 'We'll go into the water now. Come on!'

And soon the Five, Timmy too, were splashing in the sea, yelling and diving in and out, having a glorious time, while Oliver paddled near the shore.

Then suddenly Julian gave a shout, and pointed to the beach.

'Look! What's happening there? Hey!'

All the Five looked, and saw something very surprising! The two men who owned the big brown dog were dragging Oliver out of the water, one with his hand over the boy's mouth.

'They're kidnapping him! Remember that threatening letter he told us about, that his dad got this morning? Come on, quick – see if we can stop them. TIMMY! Come on, now!'

Chapter 4

They swam to the shore and slipped hurriedly into their sandals.

'They've taken the kid up the cliffs – they're at the top, look!' panted Julian. 'After them, Timmy!'

But not even Timmy could get up the cliffs in time to rescue the screaming boy. Julian was at the top first, with Timmy – just in time to see a car driving off. The big dog was galloping after it.

'Why didn't they take the dog in the car, too?' wondered Dick.

'Perhaps he's a car-sick dog?' said Anne. 'Anyway, I bet he knows where the men are going, and has been ordered to follow. If the car doesn't go too fast he can easily keep up.'

'I've got the number, anyway,' said Dick.

'Listen – I think Anne's right when she says the dog must know where the men are going,' said Julian. 'And it can't be far away if the dog has to run the whole distance.'

Timmy wasn't listening. He was sniffing the ground here and there. Then he suddenly began to trot along the cliff-road, nose to ground.

George gave a sudden exclamation. 'I know! He's sniffing the other dog's tracks – he knows his smell, and he's following it!'

'You're right! Look – let's see if he'll follow the trail properly,' said Julian. 'He might lead us to Oliver! Tell him, George. He always understands every word you say.'

'Timmy! Listen!' said George, and pointed to some paw marks made in the sandy road by the big mongrel dog. 'Follow, Timmy, follow. Understand?'

Timmy lifted his big head and looked hard at George, his ears pricked up, his head on one side. Yes – he understood.

Then, with nose to ground, he trotted swiftly away down the cliff-road, sniffing the tracks of the other dog. How did he do it? What a nose Timmy had!

'Come on,' said Dick. 'Timmy will lead us to wherever those men are taking Oliver.'

Chapter 5

Very steadily, Timmy followed the scent
down the cliff-road, turned off to the left,
trotted down a lane, swung to the right, then
to the left. He waited at the traffic lights,
and when they changed to green, he crossed
the road, and then trotted right through the
town, nose to trail!

The children padded behind in their
swimming things, Anne getting very puffed!

At the other end of the town Timmy
turned to the left and padded down a lane,
nose still on the scent! The four followed
closely.

'I'll have to have a rest soon,' panted Anne.

'Hey, that's the car that took the boy away!' exclaimed Dick, suddenly, as they passed a garage, outside which stood a black car, taking in petrol. 'The men are in it. But I can't see Oliver – and that great dog isn't anywhere about, either.'

'Well, they must have hidden Oliver somewhere not far off, and then they came back here for petrol,' said Julian. 'Go on, Tim – you're on the right trail. I expect they've left that dog in charge of the boy. I bet if anyone went near, he'd tear them to pieces!'

'And I don't want Timmy in a dogfight,' said George.

'Yes. Not so good,' said Julian, and came to a stop. Timmy, however, went on, and wouldn't come back, even though George called him.

'Obstinate thing!' said George crossly. 'Once he's following a trail nothing on earth will stop him. Well – I'm going after him in case he gets into trouble!'

'Look – Timmy's gone through that gateway,' said Anne, 'into a field. There's a shed at the bottom of it. Could Oliver be there, with the dog inside, guarding him?'

Timmy stopped suddenly and began to growl. George ran to catch hold of his collar. But Timmy wrenched himself away and raced to the shed, scraping at the wooden door. Immediately a volley of fierce barks came from the shed. The Five halted. A voice came from the shed.

'Help! Help, I'm locked in here!'

Chapter 6

'There – Timmy followed the trail correctly!' said George. 'Quick, Ju – we mustn't let him break in that door – the other dog will fly at him, and at us, too! Whatever can we do?'

It was obvious that the other dog had been left on guard, and would fling himself on anyone or anything that tried to prevent him from doing his duty.

'TIMMY! STOP THROWING YOURSELF AGAINST THAT DOOR!' yelled George. 'YOU'LL BREAK IT DOWN, AND THEN GOODNESS KNOWS WHAT'LL HAPPEN!'

As both dogs, barking fiercely, again flung themselves on it from opposite sides, the door cracked in two places – and the bottom half shook and shivered!

'Anne, George, quick, come with me!' said Julian. 'We may be attacked by that dog once he gets out! Run! We could perhaps climb that tree, look! Hurry up, for goodness' sake!'

Terrified, they all raced for the tree, and clambered up on the branches.

CRASH! The door fell to the ground, broken in half. At once the great mongrel leapt out.

But it took absolutely no notice of Timmy. It ran instead to the tree and stood below, growling fiercely.

Timmy stood staring in surprise. Why was this dog growling at the children? It was all a mistake, Timmy decided, and he must put it right.

He ran to the tree, and whined as if to say: 'It's all right. Please come down and play with us!' Then he went to the other dog, and whined to him too.

The mongrel gave a loud bark, and jumped up. He ran off a little, stopped and turned round as if saying to Timmy: 'All right – you want a game? Then so do I! You're the dog I played with this morning, aren't you? Well, come on, let's have a game!'

And, to the children's enormous astonishment the two dogs gambolled amiably together!

Chapter 7

'I feel a bit silly up here,' said Dick, climbing down. 'Come on – the war's over. Those dogs look as if they're friends for life. Let's go and get that kid.'

With the frightened boy safely in their midst, they began to walk cautiously out of the field.

The two dogs took absolutely no notice! The big mongrel had got Timmy down on the ground, and was pretending to worry him. Timmy was having the time of his life!

'Look – there's a bus going to Kirrin!' said Julian, delighted. 'Stop it! We'll get in and take Oliver back to safety while we've a chance. Timmy will just have to walk. He'll make that dog forget all about guarding Oliver!'

It wasn't very long before they were safely back in Kirrin. Oliver looked very white, but when Julian told him solemnly that it was really a very big adventure, he cheered up and began to boast!

'I was kidnapped! What will the boys at school say? But I was really scared though. Can we go and find my dad?'

Professor Humes was very thankful to see his son again, for already he had notified the police that he had disappeared. Dick gave the police the number of the men's car.

'You'll soon track that all right!' he said. 'But not as well as Tim here – he used his nose, and a very good nose it is too!'

'Woof!' said Timmy, and let his tongue hang out of his mouth.

'He says he's hot and thirsty,' said George. 'Let's buy him an ice-cream.'

'We'll ALL have the biggest ice-creams there are in the village shop,' said the

Professor, patting Timmy. 'I could do with one myself.'

'I could do with four,' said Oliver, 'so I hope you're feeling generous, Dad! Dad, Timmy's a wonder dog!'

'Well, we've always known that,' said George. 'Come on, Timmy – ICE-CREAMS!'

A LAZY
AFTERNOON

Chapter 1

'It's hot!' said Julian, fanning himself with a paper. 'What are we all going to do this afternoon?'

'Nothing!' said Dick at once. 'I feel as if I'm rapidly melting. It's even too hot to go swimming.'

'Let's have a lazy afternoon for once,' said George. 'If anyone suggests a walk or a bike ride in this heat, I'll scream.'

'Woof,' said Timmy at once. 'He's suggesting a walk, George,' said Anne, with a laugh. 'Scream!'

'Too hot even for that,' said George. 'Let's find a cool, shady place, take our books, and either read or snooze till tea-time. I'd enjoy a lazy afternoon for once.'

'Woof,' said Timmy mournfully, not agreeing at all.

'Come on, then,' said Julian. 'We'll go to that little copse we know, under those leafy trees – near that tiny stream that ripples along and makes a nice cool noise!'

'Well – I think I can just about walk there,' said Dick, and they all set off, strolling along, unable to keep up with the lively, energetic Timmy.

'It makes me hot even to look at Timmy,' complained Dick. 'Hot to hear him too, puffing like a steam-train. Put your tongue in, Timmy, I can't bear to look at it.'

Chapter 2

Timmy ran ahead, glad that they were off for what appeared to be a walk. He was very disappointed when the others flopped down in a little copse under some big leafy trees near a small brook. He stood looking at them in disgust.

'Sorry, Tim. No walkies,' said George. 'Come and sit down with us. For goodness' sake, don't go rabbiting in this weather.'

'It'd be a waste of your time, Timmy,' said Dick. 'All sensible bunnies are having an afternoon snooze, down at the bottom of their holes, waiting for the cool evening to come.'

'Woof,' said Timmy in scorn, watching the four arrange themselves comfortably under a canopy made by young saplings and bushes.

Branches from big trees nearby overhung them, and by the time the four had wriggled themselves well into the little thicket, not a single sunbeam could reach them. In fact, it was difficult to see them, so well hidden were they in the green shade.

'This is better,' said George. 'I think it's about the coolest spot we'll find anywhere. Doesn't that little stream sound nice, too, gurgling away over the stones? I think I'm going to sleep – and if you dare to flop yourself down on my middle, Timmy, I'll send you home!'

Timmy stood and looked at the well-hidden four. His tail drooped. What was the point of coming to a wood, to lie down and do nothing? Well – he was going rabbiting! He swung round, pushed his way out of the thicket, and disappeared.

George raised her head to look after him.

'He's gone rabbiting after all,' she said. 'Well, I hope he remembers where we are and comes back at tea-time. Now for a lazy – peaceful – quiet afternoon!'

'Don't talk so much,' said Dick, and got a sideways kick from George's foot.

'Oh, I feel sleepy!'

Chapter 3

In a few minutes' time not one of the
four was awake.

Books lay unopened on the ground.

A small beetle ran over Anne's bare leg,
and she didn't even feel it.

A robin hopped on to a branch just above
Dick's face, but his eyes were closed and he
didn't see it.

It certainly was a hot afternoon. Nobody
was about at all. Not a sound was to be
heard except for the running water nearby,
and a yellowhammer somewhere who
persisted in saying that he wanted 'a little
bit of bread and no cheese'. The four were as

sound asleep as if they were in bed.

And then, far away on a road that bordered the wood, a motorbike came by. It had a sidecar, and it made quite a noise. But the four sleepers heard nothing.

They didn't know that the motorbike had slowed down and turned into the wood, taking one of the grassy woodland walks that wound here and there, quiet and cool.

The motorbike came slowly down one of the paths, not making very much noise now, because it was going slowly. It came near to the little copse where the children lay hidden in the cool shade of the bushes.

The engine of the motorbike gave a sudden little cough as it came along, and Julian awoke with a start.

What was that noise? He listened, but he could hear nothing more because the motorbike, with its sidecar, had now stopped.

Julian shut his eyes again. But he opened them immediately because he heard voices – low voices. People must be somewhere near. Where were they? Julian hoped they wouldn't disturb the four in their cool hiding place. He made a little peephole in the bush he was lying under, and spied through it.

Chapter 4

Julian saw the motorbike and sidecar on the grassy path some way off. He saw two men, one just getting out of the sidecar. Julian didn't like the look of them at all.

'What nasty-looking men!' he thought. 'What are they doing here in the middle of a summer's afternoon?'

At first the men talked in low voices, and then an argument started. One raised his voice. 'I tell you, we were followed! It's the only thing to do, to come here and dump the stuff!'

A small bag was dragged out of the sidecar. The second man seemed to be grumbling, not at all willing to do what the other wanted.

'I tell you, I know it won't be found if we put it there,' said the first man. 'What's the matter with you? We can't afford to be stopped with the stuff on us – and I know we were being followed. It was only because we crossed against those traffic lights that we got away.'

Julian awoke the others, and whispered to them. Something strange was happening!

Soon all the four were peeping through leafy peepholes at what was going on.

They saw what looked like a small mailbag on the ground by the motorbike.

'What are they going to do with it?' whispered George. 'Should we burst out on them?'

'I would if we had Timmy with us,' whispered back Julian. 'But he's gone rabbiting and may be miles away.'

'And these crooks would be more than a match for us,' said Dick. 'We daren't even show ourselves. We can only watch.'

Chapter 5

'I hope we see where they hide the stuff, whatever it is,' said Anne, trying to spy through the leaves. 'There they go with the bag.'

'I can see them,' said Dick, almost forgetting to whisper in his excitement. 'They're climbing a tree!'

'Yes – one's already up, and the other's passing the bag to him,' whispered Julian. 'It must have a hollow trunk, I think. Oh, I wish Timmy was here!'

'Now the second man's trying to climb up, too,' said George. 'The first one wants help, I suppose. The bag must be stuck.'

Both men were now up the tree, trying to stuff the bag down some kind of hollow there. At last there was a thud as if the bag had dropped down.

'If only Timmy was here!' said Julian again. 'It's maddening to lie here and do nothing – but we'd be no match for those two men!'

Then a sudden noise came to their ears – the scampering of feet. Then came a familiar sound. 'Woof!'

'Timmy!' yelled Julian and George together, and Julian leapt up and pushed his way out of his hiding place at once. 'Tell Tim to guard that tree, George, quick!'

Chapter 6

'Here, Timmy – on guard!' shouted George, and the astonished Timmy ran to the tree where the two men were staring down in sudden horror.

Timmy gave a blood-curdling growl and one man, who had been about to jump down, shrank back.

'Call that dog off!' he yelled. 'What do you think you're doing?'

'You tell us what you're doing,' said Julian. 'What's in the bag you pushed down that tree hollow?'

'What bag? What are you talking about? You must be mad!' said the man. 'Call that dog off, or I'll report you to the police.'

'Right! We'll report you at the same time!' said Julian. 'You'll stay up that tree till we bring the police back here – and I warn you, if you try jumping down and running away, you'll be sorry. You've no idea what sharp teeth that dog has!'

The two men were so angry that they could hardly speak. Timmy barked loudly, and kept leaping up to try to reach them.

Julian turned to the others. 'Go to the main road and stop a car. Go to the nearest police station and tell the police there to send men here at once. Hurry up.'

But before the others could go off, there came the sound of another motorbike – and then a second – bumping along the woodland path. Julian fell silent. Were more crooks coming? Timmy would be a great help, if so. Julian and the others got behind trees and watched to see who was on the coming motorbikes.

Chapter 7

'The police!' yelled Dick, suddenly seeing the familiar uniform. 'They must have been the ones chasing those men. Somebody must have given them the tip that they had turned off into the wood! Hey! We can help you!'

The two policemen stopped in surprise. They saw the motorbike and sidecar.

'Have you kids seen anything of two men with a bag?' shouted one of them.

'Yes. The bag's stuffed down a tree over there, and our dog's guarding the men – they're up in the tree!' shouted back Julian, going towards the police. 'You've just come in time to collect them!'

'Good stuff!' said the policeman with a grin, as he saw the two scared men up the tree, with Timmy still leaping up hopefully at them. 'The bag's up there, too, is it?'

'Down in the hollow of the tree,' said Julian.

'Well, thanks very much for doing our job for us,' said the second policeman. 'We've got some pals on the main road,' he said. 'We said we'd shout if we found anything. They'll soon be along.' He looked at the two men in the tree. 'Well, Jim and Stan? You thought you'd fooled us, didn't you? Are you coming quietly – or do we ask the dog to help us round you up?'

Chapter 8

Jim and Stan took one look at the eager Timmy.

'We'll come quietly,' they said, and, when three more men came racing down the woodland path, there was no trouble at all.

Jim and Stan went off with the policemen, Timmy gave one last fierce bark, and all Five watched the men, the motorbikes, and the sidecar disappear with many bumps up the path back to the main road.

'Well!' said George. 'Talk about a nice cool, lazy afternoon! I'm hotter than ever now!'

'Woof,' said Timmy, his tongue hanging out almost to the ground. He looked very hot, too.

'Well, you shouldn't go rabbiting,' said George. 'No wonder you're hot!'

'It's a very good thing he did go rabbiting!' said Dick. 'If he'd been with us, he'd have barked, and those men would have known we were here – and would have gone further on to hide their goods. We'd never have seen what they were doing, or have been able to catch them.'

'Yes. That's true,' said George, and patted Timmy. 'All right, Timmy – you were right to go rabbiting and to come back when you did!'

'Tea-time, everybody!' said Dick, looking at his watch. 'Well – what a very nice, peaceful, lazy afternoon! I really have enjoyed it!'

WHEN TIMMY
CHASED THE CAT

Chapter 1

'What are you going to do today?' said Aunt Fanny to the Five.

They all looked up from their books – except Timmy, who looked up from the bone he was gnawing.

'We ought to go for a walk, I suppose,' said Julian. 'But the wind's so bitter today. I always think January is a pretty dreary month, unless there's snow – or we can go skating.'

'But there's no snow, and no ice – only this horrible, freezing wind,' said Anne. 'I'd just as soon stay in and read my Christmas books!'

'Oh no – we must go out,' said George at once. 'What about Timmy? He's got to have his usual walk.'

Timmy's ears pricked up at once when he heard that word. Walk! Ha – just what he was wanting! He got up at once and ran to George, whining.

She patted him. 'All right, all right, Tim – we'll leave Anne here with her books, and we'll go out for a nice long walk.'

'Would you like to go to the cinema in Beckton?' asked her mother. 'There's a good film on today, about circus life. I'll pay for you all, if you'd like to go this afternoon.'

'Mum – I think you're trying to get rid of us!' said George.

'Well – in a way I am,' said her mother, with a laugh. 'Your dad has two friends coming to see him this afternoon – and I really think it would be easier if you were out of the house.'

'Oh, I see,' said George. 'Two more of his scientist friends, I suppose. Well, I'd just as soon be out in that case. It's awful not even to be able to sneeze in case I get into trouble for making a noise.'

'Don't exaggerate, George,' said her mother. 'Well, Julian – would you like to go to the cinema?'

'Of course – and it's very kind of you to pay for us,' said Julian. 'I tell you what – we'll walk to Beckton, so that we'll give our legs a stretch – and get the train back.'

'Yes. That's a good idea,' said Dick. 'I feel as if I want a good run. Just listen to Tim thumping his tail on the ground. He thoroughly agrees!'

Chapter 2

So that afternoon, the Five set off to walk to Beckton. The wind was in their faces, and it was very cold indeed; but they were soon warm with walking, and even Anne began to enjoy striding out against the wind.

Timmy loved it, of course. He was full of high spirits, and pranced and capered and bounded about joyfully. He wagged his long tail nineteen to the dozen, chased dead leaves as if they were rats, and made everyone laugh at him.

'Dear Tim,' said Anne. 'It must be lovely to be a dog, and have four legs to leap about on, instead of just two!'

Halfway to Beckton they came to a big, rather lonely-looking house called Tarleys Mount. The gates opened on to a short drive that ran to the front steps of the house. On the top of one of the stone gateposts sat a BIG black cat. It looked disdainfully down at Timmy.

At first Timmy didn't see it, and then he suddenly caught sight of it and stopped. A cat! And a big one, too. But sadly, just out of reach!

Timmy pranced in front of the gatepost and barked loudly. The cat yawned widely, and then began to wash one of her paws, as if to say – 'A dog! Nasty smelly creature! Not worth taking notice of!'

But Timmy could leap very high, and the cat was suddenly startled to see his head appearing near the top of the gatepost as he jumped. She hissed and spat.

'Stop it, Timmy,' said George. 'You know you're not allowed to chase cats. Come here!'

The cat spat again. That was too much for Timmy, and he jumped so high that the cat

was really alarmed. She leapt right off the gatepost, and shot into the bushes at the side of the drive.

Timmy was after her in a flash, yelping madly.

George yelled, but he took no notice at all.

'Bad dog,' said Julian. 'He'll be ages chasing that cat and hunting for it. He ought to know by now that he isn't a match for any cat living!'

'I'll go in and see if I can get him,' said George. 'Hope I don't meet an angry gardener!'

'We'll come with you,' said Dick. 'Come on. I can hear Tim down the drive. He must be near the house.'

Chapter 3

They went in at the gate and down the little drive. Yes – Timmy was by the front door, barking under a tree there.

'I bet the cat's sitting on a branch making faces at him,' said Julian. 'Call him, George.'

'Timmy, Timmy! Come here at once!' shouted George. But he wouldn't.

Then just as they got up to him and George was bending down to take hold of his collar, the cat leapt down the tree and raced round the house to the back. Timmy was after her at once, yelping madly.

'Oh no!' said George, vexed. 'We'll have the people of the house out after us – they must wonder what's going on!'

They ran round the house after Timmy, and came to the back entrance. There was a little yard there, with a clothes line and two or three dustbins and a coal bunker. The cat was now sitting on top of the bunker, daring Timmy to leap up and get her.

'Now then, you dog – you leave that cat alone!' said an angry voice as the four children turned into the yard. They saw a neat little woman standing there, in a thick coat with a scarf round her head. She held a small basket in her hand, with a little bottle of milk in it and a jar.

'I'm so sorry about our dog,' said George, and pounced on Timmy. She got hold of his collar this time and spoke to him sharply. 'I'm ashamed of you! Bad dog! Very bad dog.'

Timmy's tail drooped, and he gave George's hand a very small lick. The little woman watched him, frowning.

'He gave me a real fright, that dog of yours,' she said. 'Tearing into the yard like a mad thing – first old Sooty the cat – then the dog!'

'I hope his barking didn't disturb the people in the house,' said Julian.

'What's that you say?' said the woman, cupping her hand behind her ear. 'I'm a bit deaf.'

'I SAID I HOPE HIS BARKING DIDN'T DISTURB THE PEOPLE IN THE HOUSE,' repeated Julian in a louder voice.

'Oh, they're away,' said the little woman, taking off the top of the milk bottle. 'Miss Ella went on Monday, and her old aunt went yesterday. I just came to feed the old cat. Here, Sooty – come and lap your milk, and I'll put your fish down, too. Hold that dog, please.'

She emptied some cooked fish out of the jar, and poured milk into an enamel saucer by the back doorstep. The cat sat on the coal bunker and looked down longingly, but wouldn't come near it.

'WE'LL TAKE THE DOG AND GO,' said Dick.

'What did you say?' said the woman. 'Oh yes – you go; then old Sooty will come along down. He must be hungry.'

Chapter 4

The four children went round the house
again, George holding Timmy's collar.

'Funny – I can hear somebody talking!'
said Anne, suddenly, as they went along the
drive. 'Can you, Dick?'

'Yes,' said Dick, puzzled. 'But there's
nobody about.'

They all stopped to listen. 'It sounds like a
loud conversation,' said Julian. 'Is it coming
from the house?'

'No – you heard what the woman said.
The people are away,' said George. 'It must
be somebody talking very loudly in the road.'

But the talking couldn't be heard when

they reached the gates. 'Oh well – it was probably gardeners somewhere in the trees off the drive,' said Dick. 'Come on – we'll be late for the film, if we don't hurry up.'

They were just in time for it and settled down to watch the circus story on the screen. It was very good, and they all enjoyed it thoroughly.

They collected Timmy from the kindly attendant, and he barked in welcome.

They felt very hungry, and the little café opposite looked very inviting, with its wonderful display of cakes in the window.

'Come on – I'll buy tea for everyone – providing George doesn't eat more than six cakes!' said Julian, rattling the money in his pocket. 'Timmy, I'll buy you one too.'

They had a wonderful tea, and finished up with an ice-cream each. Timmy was treated to a cake and a biscuit, and licked George's ice-cream saucer clean.

'Well – I don't know if we can manage to walk to the station now!' said Dick. 'I feel pretty full. What's the matter, George?'

'I was just feeling Timmy's collar – and he's lost his Tail Wagger badge,' said George. 'It's got his name and address on it. Oh no! I only bought him a new one last week.'

'If we want to catch the train back, we'd better get a move on,' said Julian, looking at his watch.

Chapter 5

'No, I'm going to walk home,' said George. 'I've got a torch. I may find Timmy's badge.'

'Oh, for pity's sake!' groaned Dick. 'Don't say we've got to walk back hunting for the badge all the way home. No, George – that's too much.'

'I can go alone, with Timmy,' said George. 'I didn't mean you others to come.'

'Well – we can't let you walk a mile or two home in the dark by yourself,' said Julian. 'I tell you what – I'll go with you, George, and Dick and Anne can go back by train.'

'No, thanks,' said Anne. 'I'll come too. I think I know where Tim dropped his badge. In the drive of that big house! Do you remember when the cat sat up in a tree and Timmy leapt up at her? Well, he caught his collar on a bough – and I bet that's when he lost his Tail Wagger badge.'

'Yes – I expect you're right,' said George. 'Timmy's being a bit of a nuisance today – aren't you, Tim? I hope that cat won't be anywhere about in the garden.'

'Tie a bit of string to Tim's collar,' said Dick, producing a piece. 'And hang on to him, George! Well – are we ready?'

They all set off in the starry night. They hardly needed their torches once they had got used to the dark, because the stars were so very bright.

They came at last to Tarleys Mount, and stopped at the gates.

'Here we are,' said Dick, flashing his torch. 'We know where Timmy went this morning, and if we hunt about we're pretty certain to find the badge.'

'Now, you keep by me, Tim,' said George, holding tightly to the string lead.

They all went down the drive – and in the middle of it they stopped in surprise.

'I can hear those voices again – well, different ones this time – but voices!' said Anne, astonished. 'Who can be out here, talking and talking in the night?'

'Beats me!' said Dick. 'Come on – let's go to that tree by the front door. I bet the badge will be there!'

They went to the big door, still hearing the voices somewhere away in the distance. Anne suddenly gave a cry, and bent down. 'Yes – here's the badge, just where I thought it might be. Isn't that lucky?'

'Oh good!' said George, and fixed it on Timmy's collar.

'There's somebody singing now,' said Dick, standing still and listening. 'It's really odd.'

Chapter 6

'Perhaps it's a radio somewhere,' said Anne. 'It sounds a bit like one.'

'But there's no other house near here,' said Julian. 'Not near enough for us to hear the radio, anyway.'

The singing voice stopped – and band music came on the air. 'There!' said Anne. 'That's the radio all right! There can't be any band playing in the open air this cold night.'

'You're right,' said Julian, puzzled. 'Do you think that the sounds can be coming from this house – Tarleys Mount?'

'But we know there's no one there,' said Dick. 'That woman who fed the cat this morning told us the house was empty. That's why she had to come and feed the cat. And if someone had left the radio on in the house, she'd have heard it and switched it off.'

'No, she wouldn't,' said George.

'Why not?' asked Dick, surprised.

'Well, because she was deaf!' said George. 'She kept putting her hand behind her ear, don't you remember? I think the radio is on in the house.'

'You don't think somebody's got in, and is having a good time there – eating what's left in the larder, sleeping in the beds, and listening to the radio, do you?' said Anne.

'It's a bit puzzling,' said Julian. 'I can't imagine anyone going away and leaving the radio full on – and it must be, if we can hear it out here. Perhaps we ought to look round a bit. The noise seems to come from over there – the other side of the house, not where the yard is. Let's go round there.'

There was a sudden hiss from a nearby bush, and Timmy pricked up his ears. That cat again!

'Hang on to Tim – there's the cat,' said Julian, as a black streak fled across the beam of his torch. 'Come on, now – let's go round the other side of the house.'

As soon as they turned the corner, they came to a terrace, with steps leading down to a garden only faintly to be seen in the starlight. The band music was suddenly louder there. There was now no doubt at all that it was radio music.

'Well – it's certainly coming from the house,' said Julian. 'But from which room? As far as I can see, the whole place is in darkness!'

Chapter 7

So it was! Not a chink of light showed
anywhere. Julian shone his torch on to each
window. They were all tightly shut, as if the
house were indeed empty and deserted.

'There's a tree that reaches up to that
balcony,' said Dick. 'I'll shin up and get on to
it, and see if I can spot anything in the house.
If the curtains aren't drawn there, I can
shine my torch in.'

Up the tree he went, the others shining
their torches to show him which branches to
climb.

At last he was on the balcony, his own
torch now shining brightly. There were glass

doors there, and the curtains of the room behind weren't drawn across the panes. Dick shone his torch through the glass.

'The radio's in this room, I'm sure!' he cried. 'I can hear it clearly. It's on full, too – the noise is coming through a ventilator, above the glass doors! Oh!'

'What? What is it?' cried everyone, hearing a sudden strange note in Dick's excited voice.

'There's someone in this room!' called back Dick. 'Someone lying on the floor, but I can't see clearly enough. Whoever it is isn't moving at all. I'll tap and see if they hear me.'

The others heard the sound of tapping, and then Dick's voice again. 'Yes – the person moved when I tapped. Who on earth can it be? He must be hurt, I think, but the doors are locked, so I can't get in. I'm coming down again, so shine your torches, will you?'

Dick climbed quickly down the tree, and the others crowded round him excitedly. 'We'll have to get into the house somehow,' said Dick. 'I'm sure it's someone who's hurt – or maybe ill.'

'But how did they get in?' said Julian in wonder. 'And how can we get in, for that matter?'

'We'll try all the doors to begin with,' said Dick. 'Here's a garden door. No, that's locked. Come on round to the kitchen door. I suppose that'll be locked, too.'

But it wasn't! It opened easily enough, and the Five trooped into the house, Timmy quite excited.

The noise of the radio suddenly seemed much louder as they went in.

'Come on upstairs,' said Dick. 'We'll find that balcony room. It was all in darkness, which made it seem stranger than ever!'

They ran up the wide stairs. The sound of the radio was very loud there. They listened intently.

'It's in that room over there!' shouted Dick, and ran to a half-open door. He shone his torch round, and then let the beam rest on something lying on the floor. What could it be?

Julian reached out his hand to the light switch by the door. *Click!* The light flooded

the room and everyone blinked. The radio
went on and on all the time, the dance band
playing away gaily.

Chapter 8

On the floor near the radio lay a woman. She looked old and had silvery grey hair. She was dressed in outdoor things, and her hat lay on the floor.

The children looked at her in horror – what could have happened?

At last, to their relief, they saw her eyes open, and she looked up at them. Then she tried to speak. 'Water!' she croaked.

George darted out and found a bathroom with glasses. She filled one with water and brought it back. Julian eased the old woman up into a sitting position, and George helped her to drink the water. She managed to give them a faint smile.

'So silly of me,' she said, in a faraway kind of voice. 'I was just going downstairs to leave the house by the back door, when I slipped here on the polished floor. And, and—'

She stopped for a moment, and Anne patted her hand. 'You fell and hurt yourself?' she said. 'Where?'

'I'm afraid it's my hip,' said the old lady. 'I couldn't get up off the floor. I just couldn't. So I wasn't even able to phone for help. And there was no one in the house – my niece had gone—'

'And your daily woman is deaf, so she wouldn't hear you call!' said Julian, remembering.

'Yes, yes,' said the old lady. 'I just managed to get my arm up to the radio and switched it on!

'You see, I thought someone might hear it – perhaps a policeman coming round the house at night . . .'

'How long have you been l

'Since yesterday afternoon,' said the old

lady. 'I just couldn't move, you see. I was glad I had my outdoor things on – I'd have frozen stiff last night, it was so cold! I was so thirsty, too. Not hungry. Just very, very thirsty. You dear, kind children – oh, I am so glad to see you!'

Julian switched off the radio. 'Where's the phone?' he said. 'I'll call for a doctor – and an ambulance – and you'll soon be well cared for! Don't you worry!'

The Five stayed with her until the doctor came and, later on, the ambulance. Then Julian turned out all the lights that had been switched on, and they went into the hall. Julian slammed the front door after them.

'Come on, Timmy – keep by my side,' ordered George. 'No more cat-chasing for you!'

'What's he saying, George?' asked Anne.

George chuckled. 'He says, "Don't talk to me like that, George – if it hadn't been for me chasing that cat today, you'd never have had this little adventure."'

'Well, Timmy's right, as usual,' said

Dick. 'And if chasing a cat leads to saving somebody's life, I'm all for it. Good old Tim!'

If you've enjoyed these stories about
THE FAMOUS FIVE, turn over for an exciting extract
from the first book, *Five on Treasure Island*.

George and her cousins are on their first visit together to Kirrin Island . . .

THE FOUR children stared out to sea. They had all been so interested in exploring the exciting old castle that not one of them had noticed the sudden change in the weather.

Another rumble came. It sounded like a big dog growling in the sky. Tim heard it and growled back, sounding like a small roll of thunder himself.

'My goodness, we're in for it now,' said George, half-alarmed. 'We can't get back in time, that's certain. It's blowing up at top speed. Did you ever see such a change in the sky?'

The sky had been blue when they started. Now it was overcast, and the clouds seemed to hang very low indeed. They scudded along as if someone was chasing them – and the wind howled round in such a mournful way that Anne felt quite frightened.

'It's beginning to rain,' said Julian, feeling an enormous drop spatter on his outstretched hand. 'We had better shelter, hadn't we, George? We shall get wet through.'

'Yes, we will in a minute,' said George. 'I say, just look at these big waves coming! My word, it really *is* going to be a storm. Golly – what a flash of lightning!'

The waves were certainly beginning to run very high indeed. It was amazing to see what a change had come over them. They swelled up, turned over as soon as they came to rocks, and then rushed up the beach of the island with a great roar.

'I think we'd better pull our boat up higher still,' said George suddenly. 'It's going to be a very bad storm indeed. Sometimes these sudden summer storms are worse than a winter one.'

She and Julian ran to the other side of the island where they had left the boat. It was a good thing they went, for great waves were already racing right up to it. The two children pulled the boat up almost to the top of the low cliff and George tied it to a stout gorse bush growing there.

By now the rain was simply pelting down, and George and Julian were soaked. 'I hope the others have been sensible enough to shelter in that room that has a roof and walls,' said George.

They were there all right, looking rather cold and scared. It was very dark there, for the only light came through the two slits of windows and the small doorway.

'Could we light a fire to make things a bit more cheerful?' said Julian, looking round. 'I wonder where we can find some nice dry sticks?'

Almost as if they were answering the question a small crowd of jackdaws cried out wildly as they circled in the storm. 'Chack, chack, chack!'

'Of course! There are plenty of sticks on the ground below the tower!' cried Julian. 'You know – where the jackdaws nest. They've dropped lots of sticks there.'

He dashed out into the rain and ran to the tower. He picked up an armful of sticks and ran back.

'Good,' said George. 'We'll be able to make a nice fire with those. Anyone got any paper to start it – or matches?'

'I've got some matches,' said Julian. 'But nobody's got paper.'

'Yes,' said Anne, suddenly. 'The sandwiches are wrapped in paper. Let's undo them, and then we can use the paper for the fire.'

'Good idea,' said George. So they undid the sandwiches, and put them neatly on a broken stone, rubbing it clean first. Then they built up a fire, with the paper underneath and the sticks arranged criss-cross on top.

It was fun when they lit the paper. It flared up and the sticks at once caught fire, for they were very old and dry. Soon there was a fine cracking fire going and the little ruined room was lit by dancing flames. It was very dark outside now, for the clouds hung almost low enough to touch the top of the castle tower! And how they raced by! The wind sent them off to the north-east, roaring behind them with a noise like the sea itself.

'I've never, never heard the sea making such an awful noise,' said Anne. 'Never! It really sounds as if it's shouting at the top of its voice.'

What with the howling of the wind and the crashing of the great waves all round the little island, the children could hardly hear themselves speak! They had to shout at one another.

'Let's have our dinner!' yelled Dick, who was feeling terribly hungry as usual. 'We can't do anything much while this storm lasts.'

'Yes, let's,' said Anne, looking longingly at the ham sandwiches. 'It will be fun to have a picnic round the fire in this dark old room. I wonder how long ago other people had a meal here? I wish I could see them.'

'Well, I don't,' said Dick, looking round half-scared as if he expected to see the old-time people walk in to share their picnic. 'It's quite a strange enough day without wanting things like that to happen.'

They all felt better when they were eating the sandwiches and drinking the ginger-beer. The fire flared up as more and more sticks caught, and gave out quite a pleasant warmth, for now that the wind had got up so strongly, the day had become cold.

'We'll take it in turns to fetch sticks,' said George.

But Anne didn't want to go alone. She was trying her best not to show that she was afraid of the storm – but it was more than she could do to go out of the cosy room into the rain and thunder by herself.

Tim didn't seem to like the storm either. He sat close by George, his ears cocked, and growled whenever the thunder rumbled. The children fed him with titbits and he ate them eagerly, for he was hungry too.

All the children had four biscuits each. 'I think I shall give all mine to Tim,' said George. 'I didn't bring him any of his own biscuits, and he does seem so hungry.'

'No, don't do that,' said Julian. 'We'll each give him a biscuit – that will be four for him – and we'll still have three left each. That will be plenty for us.'

'You are really nice,' said George. 'Tim, don't you think they are nice?'

Tim did. He licked everyone and made them laugh. Then he rolled over on his back and let Julian tickle him underneath.

The children fed the fire and finished their picnic. When it came to Julian's turn to get more sticks, he disappeared out of the room into the storm. He stood and looked around, the rain wetting his bare head.

The storm seemed to be right overhead now. The lightning flashed and the thunder crashed at the same moment. Julian was not a bit afraid of storms, but he couldn't help feeling rather over-awed at this one. It was so magnificent. The lightning tore the sky in half almost every minute, and the thunder crashed so loudly that it sounded almost as if mountains were falling down all around!

The sea's voice could be heard as soon as the thunder stopped – and that was magnificent to hear too. The spray flew so high into the air that it wetted Julian as he stood in the centre of the ruined castle.

'I really must see what the waves are like,' thought the boy. 'If the spray flies right over me here, they must be simply enormous!'

He made his way out of the castle and climbed up on to part of the ruined wall that had once run all round the castle. He stood up there, looking out to the open sea. And what a sight met his eyes!

The waves were like great walls of grey-green! They dashed over the rocks that lay all around the island, and spray flew from them, gleaming white in the stormy sky. They rolled up to the island and dashed themselves against it with such terrific force that Julian could feel the wall beneath his feet tremble with the shock.

The boy looked out to sea, marvelling at the really great sight he saw. For half a moment he wondered if the sea might come right over the island itself? Then he knew that couldn't happen, for it would have happened before. He stared at the great waves coming in – and then he saw something rather strange.

There was something else out on the sea by the rocks besides the waves – something dark, something big, something that seemed to lurch out of the waves and settle down again. What could it be?

'It can't be a ship,' said Julian to himself, his heart beginning to beat fast as he strained his eyes to see through the rain and the spray. 'And yet it looks more like a ship than anything else. I hope it isn't a ship. There wouldn't be anyone saved from it on this dreadful day!'

He stood and watched for a while. The dark shape heaved into sight again and then sank away once more. Julian decided to go and tell the others. He ran back to the firelit room.

'George! Dick! There's something strange out on the rocks beyond the island!' he shouted, at the top of his voice. 'It looks like a ship – and yet it can't possibly be. Come and see!'

The others stared at him in surprise, and jumped to their feet. George hurriedly flung some more sticks on the fire to keep it going, and then she and the others quickly followed Julian out into the rain.

The storm seemed to be passing over a little now. The rain was not pelting down quite so hard. The thunder was rolling a little farther off, and the lightning did not flash so often. Julian led the way to the wall on which he had climbed to watch the sea.

Everyone climbed up to gaze out to sea. They saw a great tumbled, heaving mass of grey-green water, with waves rearing up everywhere. Their tops broke over the rocks and they rushed up to the island as if they would gobble it whole. Anne slipped her arm through Julian's. She felt rather small and scared.

'You're all right, Anne,' said Julian, loudly. 'Now just watch – you'll see something strange in a minute.'

They all watched. At first they saw nothing, for the waves reared up so high that they hid everything a little way out. Then suddenly George saw what Julian meant.

'Gracious!' she shouted. 'It *is* a ship! Yes, it is! Is it being wrecked? It's a big ship – not a sailing-boat, or fishing-smack!'

'Oh, is anyone in it?' wailed Anne.

The four children watched and Tim began to bark as he saw the strange dark shape lurching here and there in the enormous waves. The sea was bringing the ship nearer to shore.

'It will be dashed on to those rocks,' said Julian, suddenly. 'Look – there it goes!'

As he spoke there came a tremendous crashing, splintering sound, and the dark shape of the ship settled down on to the sharp teeth of the dangerous rocks on the south-west side of the island. It stayed there, shifting only slightly as the big waves ran under it and lifted it a little.

'She's stuck there,' said Julian. 'She won't move now. The sea will soon be going down a bit, and then the ship will find herself held by those rocks.'

As he spoke, a ray of pale sunshine came wavering out between a gap in the thinning clouds. It was gone almost at once. 'Good!' said Dick, looking upwards. 'The sun will be out again soon. We can warm ourselves then and get dry – and maybe we can find out what that poor ship is. Oh, Julian – I do so hope there was nobody in it. I hope they've all taken to boats and got safely to land.'

The clouds thinned out a little more. The wind stopped roaring and dropped to a steady breeze. The sun shone out again for a longer time, and the children felt its welcome warmth. They all stared at the ship on the rocks. The sun shone on it and lighted it up.

'There's something odd about it somehow,' said

Julian, slowly. 'Something awfully odd. I've never seen a ship quite like it.'

George was staring at it with a strange look in her eyes. She turned to face the three children, and they were astonished to see the bright gleam in her blue eyes. The girl looked almost too excited to speak.

'What is it?' asked Julian, catching hold of her hand.

'Julian – oh, Julian – it's my wreck!' she cried, in a high excited voice. 'Don't you see what's happened? The storm has lifted the ship up from the bottom of the sea, and has lodged it on those rocks. It's my wreck!'

The others saw at once that she was right. It was the old wrecked ship! No wonder it looked peculiar. No wonder it looked so old and dark, and such a strange shape. It was the wreck, lifted high out of its sleeping-place and put on the rocks nearby.

'George! We shall be able to row out and get into the wreck now!' shouted Julian. 'We shall be able to explore it from end to end. We may find the boxes of gold. Oh, *George*!'

Get to know Timothy

Timothy is a big brown mongrel dog. He is George's soulmate – they've been inseparable since she found him as a puppy on the moor. But for quite some time, she had to keep him a secret from her parents. Timmy can be boisterous when he is being friendly, but he can also be fierce and alarming when he's angered. He can even frighten other dogs, such as Tinker, the Stick family's pet – although he is fond of many animals, like Trotter, the milkman's horse. Criminals think he is an easy target but they underestimate his cleverness and his loyalty to the rest of the Five. He loves to roam free and hates being locked up on car journeys or train rides, although he enjoys riding out to sea in boats.

Other people say

As a dog, Timothy was far from perfect. He was the wrong shape, his head was too big, his ears were too pricked, his tail was too long. But he was such a mad, friendly, clumsy, laughable creature that every one of the children adored him at once.

He never minds how far we run.

Timmy says

WOOF!

Enid Blyton

is one of the most popular children's authors of all time.
Her books have sold over 500 million copies and have been
translated into other languages more often than any other
children's author.

Enid Blyton adored writing for children. She wrote over
600 books and hundreds of short stories. *The Famous Five*
books, now 75 years old, are her most popular. She is also the
author of other favourites including *The Secret Seven*,
The Magic Faraway Tree, *Malory Towers* and *Noddy*.

Born in London in 1897, Enid lived much of her life in
Buckinghamshire and adored dogs, gardening and the
countryside. She was very knowledgeable about trees, flowers,
birds and animals. Dorset – where some of the Famous Five's
adventures are set – was a
favourite place of
hers too.

Enid Blyton's stories
are read and loved by
millions of children
(and grown-ups) all
over the world.
Visit enidblyton.com
to discover more.

CELEBRATING

WORLD
**BOOK
DAY**

20
2 MARCH
2017

BOOK IN
FOR YOUR NEW ADVENTURE TODAY

3 brilliant ways to continue YOUR reading adventure

1 VISIT YOUR LOCAL BOOKSHOP

Your go-to destination for awesome reading recommendations and events with your favourite authors and illustrators.

**Booksellers.org.uk/
bookshopsearch**

2 JOIN YOUR LOCAL LIBRARY

Browse and borrow from a huge selection of books, get expert ideas of what to read next, and take part in wonderful family reading activities – all for FREE!

FIND
YOUR LOCAL
LIBRARY

Findalibrary.co.uk

3 DISCOVER A WORLD OF STORIES ONLINE

32 podcasts to try

Stuck for ideas of what to read next? Plug yourself in to our brilliant new podcast library! Sample a world of amazing books, brought to life by amazing storytellers. **worldbookday.com**

HAPPY BIRTHDAY WORLD BOOK DAY!

WORLD
BOOK
DAY
20
2 MARCH 2017

Let's celebrate . . .

Can you believe this year is our **20th birthday** – and thanks to you, as well as our amazing authors, illustrators, booksellers, librarians and teachers, there's SO much to celebrate!

Did you know that since WORLD BOOK DAY began in 1997, we've given away over **275 million book tokens**? WOW! We're delighted to have brought so many books directly into the hands of millions of children and young people just like you, with a gigantic assortment of fun activities and events and resources and quizzes and dressing-up and games too – we've even broken a **Guinness World Record**!

Whether you love discovering books that make you **laugh**, CRY, *hide under the covers* or **drive your imagination wild**, with WORLD BOOK DAY, there's always something for everyone to choose–as well as ideas for exciting new books to try at bookshops, libraries and schools everywhere.

And as a small charity, we couldn't do it without a lot of help from our friends in the publishing industry and our brilliant sponsor, NATIONAL BOOK TOKENS. Hip-hip hooray to them and three cheers to you, our readers and everyone else who has joined us over the last 20 years to make WORLD BOOK DAY happen.

Happy Birthday to us – and happy reading to you!

Illustrations © Liz Pichon

SPONSORED BY

NATIONAL BOOK tokens

#WorldBookDay20